PARALLEL LIVES

RACHEL CARSON

Born in 1907

FRIDA KAHLO

Julie Knutson

CHERRY LAKE PRESS

Published in the United States of America by Cherry Lake Publishing
Ann Arbor, Michigan
www.cherrylakepublishing.com

Reading Adviser: Marla Conn, MS, Ed., Literacy specialist, Read-Ability, Inc.
Cover Designer: Felicia Macheske

Photo Credits: © Courtesy of U.S. Fish &Wildlife Service, cover, 1 [left]; © Wikimedia Commons/Guillermo Kahlo/CC0 1.0 Universal/Public Domain Dedication, cover, 2 [right]; © Everett Historical/Shutterstock.com, 5; © Library of Congress, HAER CAL,19-LONGB,2-A—91, 6; © Library of Congress, LC-DIG-det-4a10410, 9; © chrisdorney/Shutterstock.com, 10; © Rhs/AP/Shutterstock.com, 12; © Library of Congress, LC-DIG-highsm- 45818, 15; © Rejean Bedard/iStock.com, 16; © Marketa Novakova/Dreamstime.com, 19; © Transcendental Graphics/Getty Images, 21; © Library of Congress, LC-USZ62-42516, 22; © Everett Collection/Shutterstock.com, 24; © Fine Arts Images/agefotostock.com, 25; © Library of Congress, LC-DIG-ds-05049, 26

Library of Congress Cataloging-in-Publication Data

Names: Knutson, Julie, author.
Title: Born in 1907 : Rachel Carson and Frida Kahlo / by Julie Knutson.
Description: Ann Arbor, Michigan : Cherry Lake Publishing, [2020] | Series: Parallel lives | Includes bibliographical references and index. | Audience: Grades: 4-6
Identifiers: LCCN 2019033402 (print) | LCCN 2019033403 (ebook) | ISBN 9781534159181 (hardcover) | ISBN 9781534161481 (paperback) | ISBN 9781534160330 (pdf) | ISBN 9781534162631 (ebook)
Subjects: LCSH: Carson, Rachel, 1907-1964—Juvenile literature. | Kahlo, Frida—Juvenile literature. | Women—North America—Biography—Juvenile literature. | Women environmentalists—United States—Biography—Juvenile literature. | Women painters—Mexico—Biography—Juvenile literature. | Nineteen-o-seven, A.D.—Juvenile literature. | North America—Social conditions—20th century—Juvenile literature. | North America—History—20th century—Juvenile literature.
Classification: LCC E36 .K68 2020 (print) | LCC E36 (ebook) | DDC 333.95/16092 [B]—dc23
LC record available at https://lccn.loc.gov/2019033402
LC ebook record available at https://lccn.loc.gov/2019033403

Cherry Lake Publishing would like to acknowledge the work of the Partnership for 21st Century Learning, a Network of Battelle for Kids. Please visit www.battelleforkids.org/networks/p21 for more information.

Printed in the United States of America
Corporate Graphics

ABOUT THE AUTHOR

Julie Knutson shares a birth year with Venus Williams, Chelsea Clinton, and Lin-Manuel Miranda. An avid student of history and former teacher, she lives in northern Illinois with her husband and son.

TABLE OF CONTENTS

CHAPTER 1

Welcome to 1907 4

CHAPTER 2

Rachel Carson (b. May 27, 1907) 8

CHAPTER 3

Frida Kahlo (b. July 6, 1907) 18

TIMELINE 28-29

RESEARCH AND ACT 30

FURTHER READING 30

GLOSSARY 31

INDEX 32

CHAPTER 1

Welcome to 1907

1907. **Environmentalist**-writer Rachel Carson and artist Frida Kahlo are born. In this year, the United States saw record **immigration** from Europe. Women worldwide demanded voting rights. **Muckraking** journalists exposed dishonest businesses. They were supported by **progressive** reformers seeking to address **inequality**. Cities were growing, and the countryside was shrinking. For some, new inventions like the electric washing machine revolutionized home life. Major developments in politics and technology influenced the lives and voices of these two women.

Women's Rights: Rachel and Frida were born during a time that didn't guarantee equality for men and women in politics,

There was a lot of opposition from both women and men to women's right to vote.

Henry Ford invented the Model T in 1908. His assembly line forever changed the way goods would be made.

education, or work. In schools, girls often only took classes that prepared them for life as mothers and homemakers. Only men had a role in public life. **Suffragists** sought to change this by fighting for women's voting rights and, by extension, the right to participate in public life. In the United States, women gained the right to vote in 1920. In Mexico, it didn't happen until 1953.

Industrialization and Urbanization: Rachel and Frida lived in a time of new technologies, changing work patterns, and shifting population centers. In the decades before their births, **industrialization** had forever changed how and where people lived. With industrialization, goods were no longer handmade on a small scale. Now they were mass produced in factories, which were largely concentrated in **urban** areas. Since these factories offered jobs, many people migrated to cities. In the United States, the number of people living in cities jumped from 15.3 percent in 1850 to 39.7 percent by 1900. This trend continued throughout the 20th century. In response to these changes, **conservationists** called for the need to protect public lands and wildlife.

What Do We Mean By "Voice"?

"Voice" refers to a person's view of the world and willingness to express it. Each individual's voice is shaped by their unique experiences. People exercise voice in different ways, from political protest to public speaking to visual art.

CHAPTER 2

Rachel Carson (b. May 27, 1907)

From a young age, Rachel Carson combined her passion for writing with her love of nature. As an adult, she harnessed these twin interests to educate the public about environmental issues. In the process, she changed the way we think about how human choices impact the planet.

Silent Spring

"If we are going to live so intimately with these chemicals—eating and drinking them, taking them into the very marrow of our bones—we had better know something about their power."

— *Rachel Carson,* Silent Spring

Rachel's book, *Silent Spring*, got people thinking about the impact of industry on nature.

Beatrix Potter self-published *The Tale of Peter Rabbit* in 1901.

Early Years: Finding a Voice

Rachel's outlook on the world was influenced by a few key figures and experiences. She spent her earliest years exploring her family's 64-acre (26 hectares) farm in Springdale, Pennsylvania, alongside her mother, Maria. The family's orchards were her first classrooms; their chickens, pigs, and dogs were her first classmates. Here, Rachel learned the power of observation. She and her mother watched and listened to birds and insects. Together, they treasured stories about nature and animals. Beatrix Potter was a favorite author.

As a child, Rachel witnessed the impact of industry on her small community. As Rachel grew, so did the presence of factories in the town. A glue factory, power company, and lighting manufacturer moved to Springdale, forever altering its smell, sounds, look, and feel. The Carsons took a stand against this shift. Although they weren't wealthy and needed money, her father refused to sell portions of their farm to a coal company, fearing it would damage the land.

Middle Years: Expressing a Voice

In the mid-1920s, the field of science was dominated by men, but Rachel wanted to be a scientist. Family, friends, and teachers warned her that, as a woman, it might be hard to find a job. But that didn't stop her. She graduated from the Pennsylvania College for Women with a degree in biology. She then went on to study at Johns Hopkins University in Baltimore, Maryland, earning a master's degree in zoology with a focus on marine science.

Rachel Carson was the first woman to be awarded a National Book Award in nonfiction.

Rachel finished her degree in 1932, but the timing wasn't ideal. The United States was deep in the **Great Depression**, with nearly 24 percent of Americans out of work. Rachel needed a job, but jobs were in short supply. A former professor encouraged her to take the civil service exam, a test for government jobs. She scored better than all the other applicants and became the first woman to pass the exam. As a result, Rachel secured a full-time post with the U.S. Bureau of Fisheries in 1936 as a junior biologist.

During this time, Rachel also wrote for newspapers and magazines. She published three popular science books about the sea and won a National Book Award for her work. Rachel did all this while working full-time and acting as a caregiver for her mother and two nieces.

Later Years: Leaving a Legacy

In the mid-1940s, Rachel became concerned about use of the **pesticide** dichloro-diphenyl-trichloroethane (DDT). DDT was developed to kill insects, but Rachel saw that it harmed other creatures and damaged entire **ecosystems**. While she hoped that someone else would sound the alarm on DDT, she was pushed into action by a letter she received in January 1958. Rachel's friend Olga Huckins had written to report that she'd found several birds dead after the area around her home was sprayed for mosquitos. Huckins asked Rachel if there was something she could do—or someone she could contact—in Washington, D.C., to stop the spraying.

Rachel was determined to make people aware of the unintended effects of pesticides. She continued researching and writing. Four years later, her book *Silent Spring* was released in 1962. Pesticide producers attacked Rachel, calling her a "**hysterical** woman." *TIME* magazine labeled the book "an emotional and inaccurate outburst." But science was on Rachel's side. In 1963, a presidential advisory committee confirmed *Silent Spring*'s findings. As a result,

The title of Rachel's book, *Silent Spring*, refers to what would happen if birds kept dying because of DDT.

Although they almost went completely extinct, by 2007 the bald eagle population had recovered and was removed from the endangered species list.

the Environmental Protection Agency was formed. State legislatures also acted. By the end of 1962, more than 40 states adopted laws regulating pesticides. Evidence grew against the use of DDT. In the United States, the substance was officially banned in 1972 and labeled as a **carcinogen**.

Rachel died in 1964. But her influence lives on. The Endangered Species Act was passed a year after DDT was banned, and populations of bald eagles, who were once threatened by the pesticide, made a comeback. Even *TIME* changed its tune: in 1999, the magazine named her one of the century's 100 most important people.

DDT in the Spotlight

During and after World War II, DDT was promoted as a "wonder chemical" that stopped diseases like malaria and typhus in their tracks. Its inventor even won a Nobel Prize in 1948. It was widely used by farmers to protect crops from pests. Between 1942 and 1972, approximately 675,000 tons of DDT were applied to U.S. farm fields. Today, it is still used in some African countries to combat malaria, where health officials argue that the benefits of exposure outweigh the risks.

CHAPTER 3

Frida Kahlo (b. July 6, 1907)

Frida Kahlo expressed her unique way of looking at life through brushstrokes. She is best-known for her self-portraits, and her art provides a mirror of her experiences. Frida started painting after a disabling accident at the age of 18. During her 2-year recovery period, painting allowed her to reflect on *who* she was and *what* she felt. Her self-portraits demonstrate that there's no such thing as a simple truth, and that people can live out and express a range of different identities.

Early Years: Finding a Voice

Like Rachel Carson, Frida's voice was shaped by her early circumstances. Her father, Guillermo Kahlo, was a government photographer who traveled throughout Mexico to document its buildings and landscapes. He shared his work with the young

Frida's artwork continues to inspire today. In 2016, one of her paintings sold for $8 million.

Frida, teaching her about the country's culture and history. He also encouraged her love of nature and the outdoors. Unlike many parents at the time, Guillermo also encouraged his daughter's independence. Frida could be Frida; she didn't need to be like everyone else.

At the age of 6, Frida got sick with **polio**. She was unable to get out of bed and was out of school for 9 months. Even after she recovered, polio left its mark. One of her legs was thin and weak, and other children teased her for it. She hid it under clothing and layers of socks, never wanting to be pitied or thought weak. Despite her disability, she swam, played soccer, wrestled, and boxed.

At age 15, Frida set off for the National Preparatory School in Mexico City. Of the school's more than 2,000 students, she was 1 of only 35 girls. Frida was studious, persistent, and politically active. She loved science and wanted to become a doctor. She was

Revolution!

The Mexican Revolution began in November 1910, 3 years after Frida's birth. At that time, land and power were controlled by a small fraction of Mexicans, most of whom had European ancestors. The majority of people of **indigenous** *and* **mestizo** *heritage worked for these rich landowners, but held no property of their own. The revolution aimed to fix this by redistributing the land to those who actually worked it.*

The revolution lasted until 1920. Afterward, the new government strived to build cultural pride and a shared sense of identity. Leaders used art to educate the public about Mexico's past, present, and future.

Las Soldaderas were women warriors during the Mexican Revolution. They served as nurses, soldiers, and spies.

Frida married Diego in 1929.

also mischievous, and she and her friends frequently played pranks. These tricks got her expelled briefly, but she managed to talk her way back into the respected academy.

On September 17, 1925, Frida and her boyfriend were riding the bus home from school when it collided with a streetcar. Several people died. A metal armrest pierced Frida's body, leaving her with a fractured pelvis, collarbone, ribs, and legs. She was wrapped in a cast and, once again, unable to get out of bed for months.

During this long recovery period, art helped Frida heal. She borrowed her father's paints and art supplies. A special easel was made for her bed, and a mirror was placed above it so that Frida could paint her own image. From that bed, she realized that art was the path she wanted to pursue.

Middle Years: Expressing a Voice

By the end of 1927, Frida was back on her feet. She painted portraits of family members and friends and socialized with politically minded artists. She asked one of the country's best-known painters, Diego Rivera, for his opinion about her work. The two became close, and together they shaped cultural, intellectual, and political attitudes, within and beyond Mexico.

Mexicanidad

Frida Kahlo and Diego Rivera's artwork promoted the idea of "Mexicanidad," pride in Mexico's **pre-Columbian** *past and mestizo heritage. Painting was one way to visualize a shared national identity that blended many cultural traditions and influences.*

During her life, Frida Kahlo was paid the most money for her painting *The Two Fridas.*

Frida's life was always on the canvas. As she traveled, she made sense of her experiences through art. Her 1932 painting *Self-Portrait on the Borderline Between Mexico and the United States* contrasts the two countries. Mexico's soil grows fruits and flowers, while the United States has machines. The landscape of Mexico is filled with history, while industry fills the United States. Placing herself between the settings reveals conflicts that are personal, cultural, and political. The painting also speaks to big social and economic shifts of the time period. It begs the viewer to question what is lost when we move toward a world of machines.

Her painting *Self-Portrait on the Borderline Between Mexico and the United States* was completed in 1932.

Frida Kahlo is most known for her self-portraits.
She completed 55 of them in her lifetime.

Later Years: Leaving a Legacy

Throughout the 1930s, Frida's reputation grew. Shows in New York City and Paris, France, introduced her work to international audiences. Critics often tried to group her with **surrealist** artists. But Frida rejected this label, stating, "I don't paint dreams or nightmares. I paint my own reality."

Frida didn't simply exercise her views on *Mexicanidad* through her own art. She also taught up to 12 classes a week. As her health declined, her students—who called themselves *Los Fridos*—came to her house for lessons. She also served as a cultural ambassador, promoting Mexican art globally.

Despite her recognition in North America and Europe, a solo show of Frida's work had never taken place in Mexico. That changed in April 1953. Days before the opening, Frida's doctor said she was too sick to leave her bed. Rather than skip the event, Frida had her bed moved to the art gallery. She arrived by ambulance and took part in the festivities from her bed. Just more than a year later, Frida died at the age of 47. Until the end of her life, she spoke for and represented herself.

1907 · 1910 · 1920 · 1930

May 27, 1907
Rachel Carson is born in Pennsylvania.

July 6, 1907
Frida Kahlo is born in Coyoacán, Mexico City.

1910
The Mexican Revolution begins.

1914
Frida is sickened by the polio virus.

September 1918
Rachel's first story is published by *St. Nicholas Magazine*.

1925
Frida suffers severe injuries in a bus accident.

1929
Rachel graduates from the Pennsylvania College for Women with a degree in biology.

1929
Frida marries painter Diego Rivera.

1932
Rachel earns her master's degree from Johns Hopkins University.

1936
Rachel gets a job with the U.S. Bureau of Fisheries.

1938 1948 1950 1960 1972

1938
Frida's work is exhibited in New York City.

1939
The Louvre, a famous art museum in Paris, buys Frida's painting, *The Frame*.

1948
Paul Hermann Müller is awarded the Nobel Prize in Physiology or Medicine for the discovery of DDT.

1953
Frida's first solo exhibition in Mexico opens in April.

1954
Frida dies in Mexico City.

1962
Silent Spring is published.

1963
The president's Science Advisory Committee verifies the findings of *Silent Spring*.

1964
Rachel dies in Silver Spring, Maryland.

1972
DDT is banned in the United States.

Research and Act

Rachel Carson and Frida Kahlo both used their knowledge and talents to change the way people thought and acted. They revolutionized the possibilities for women in science and art. Through their work, they reshaped the world into which they were born.

Research
How are today's environmentalists and artists using their voices to change the world? What issues matter most to them? Research organizations like the Youth Climate Strike or arts collectives like the Guerrilla Girls. Map the who, what, when, where, why, and how of this group.

Act
How are people in your community improving the world? What can you do? Research nearby environmental and arts organizations. Contact them to learn more about how young people can support their efforts.

Further Reading

Alvarez, Mateo. *Frida Kahlo: Famous Mexican Artist.* New York, NY: Enslow Publishing, 2016.

Fabiny, Sarah. *Who Was Frida Kahlo?* New York, NY: Grosset & Dunlap, 2013.

Hile, Lori. *Rachel Carson: Environmental Pioneer.* Chicago, IL: Heinemann Library, 2015.

Hustad, Douglas. *Environmentalist Rachel Carson.* Minneapolis, MN: Lerner Publications, 2016.

Nardo, Don. *Frida Kahlo.* Detroit, MI: Lucent Books, 2013.

GLOSSARY

carcinogen (kahr-SIN-oh-jin) cancer-causing substance

conservationists (kahn-sur-VAY-shuhn-ists) people working to preserve land and wildlife

ecosystems (EE-koh-sis-tuhmz) all the living things in places and their relation to their environments

environmentalist (en-vye-ruhn-MENT-tuhl-ist) someone who works to protect the natural surroundings of living things, such as the air, land, and sea

Great Depression (GRAYT dih-PRESH-uhn) period of global economic stress spanning from 1929 to 1939

hysterical (hih-STER-ih-kuhl) very excited, frightened, or angry

immigration (im-uh-GRAY-shuhn) moving from one country to another to settle there

indigenous (in-DIJ-uh-nuhs) native to a place

industrialization (in-duhs-tree-uhl-ih-ZAY-shuhn) the development of industry and manufacturing

inequality (in-ih-KWAH-lih-tee) differences that seem unfair between people or things

mestizo (muh-STEE-zoh) mixed indigenous and European heritage

muckraking (MUK-rake-ing) the act of publishing articles that expose dishonest people and businesses

pesticide (PES-tih-side) a chemical used to kill pests such as insects

polio (POH-lee-oh) virus that can lead to paralysis

pre-Columbian (pree-kuh-LUM-bee-uhn) before the arrival of Europeans in the Americas

progressive (pruh-GRES-iv) people in favor of improvement or reform, especially in political or social matters

suffragists (SUHF-rij-ists) women who fought for the right to vote

surrealist (suh-REEL-ist) art and literary movement focused on exploring the unconscious mind

urban (UR-buhn) having to do with, or living in, a city

INDEX

art, 4, 18–27

bald eagles, 16, 17
Bureau of Fisheries, U.S., 13

Carson, Rachel, 4, 8–17
  awards, 12, 13
  early years, 10–13
  education, 11, 13
  legacy, 14
  middle years, 11–13
  Silent Spring, 8, 9, 14, 15
  as writer, 13
conservation, 7

DDT, 14, 15, 17

endangered species, 16, 17
Environmental Protection Agency (EPA), 17
environmentalism, 4, 8–17
equality, 4

Great Depression, 13

immigration, 4
industrialization, 7, 9, 11
inequality, 4

Kahlo, Frida, 4, 18–27
  early years, 18–23
  education, 20, 22
  legacy, 27
  middle years, 23–25
  paintings, 24–25
  self-portraits, 18, 24, 26
  as teacher, 27

"Mexicanidad," 23, 27
Mexico, 6, 18–27
muckraking, 4

National Book Award, 12, 13
nature. *See* environmentalism

observation, 10

painting, 18–27
pesticides, 14, 17
polio, 19–20
progressive reformers, 4
public lands, 7

Rivera, Diego, 22, 23

Self-Portrait on the Borderline Between Mexico and the United States, 24–25
self-portraits, 18, 24, 26
Silent Spring, 8, 9, 14, 15
suffragists, 6
surrealists, 27

timeline, 28–29

urbanization, 7

voice, 7
voting, 4, 5, 6

wildlife, 7
women's rights, 4–6